For Kate, who made everyone feel welcome

Cataloging-in-Publication Data has been applied for and may be obtained from the Library of Congress.

ISBN 978-1-4197-4417-4

CUBBY HILL is a trademark of Hasbro and is used with permission.
© Hasbro 2020
Book design by Pamela Notarantonio

Printed and bound in U.S.A.
10 9 8 7 6 5 4 3 2 1

Abrams Books for Young Readers are available at special discounts when purchased in quantity for
premiums and promotions as well as fundraising or educational use. Special editions can also be created
to specification. For details, contact specialsales@abramsbooks.com or the address below.

Abrams® is a registered trademark of Harry N. Abrams, Inc.

ABRAMS The Art of Books
195 Broadway, New York, NY 10007
abramsbooks.com

The Welcome Wagon

A Cubby Hill Tale

Cori Doerrfeld

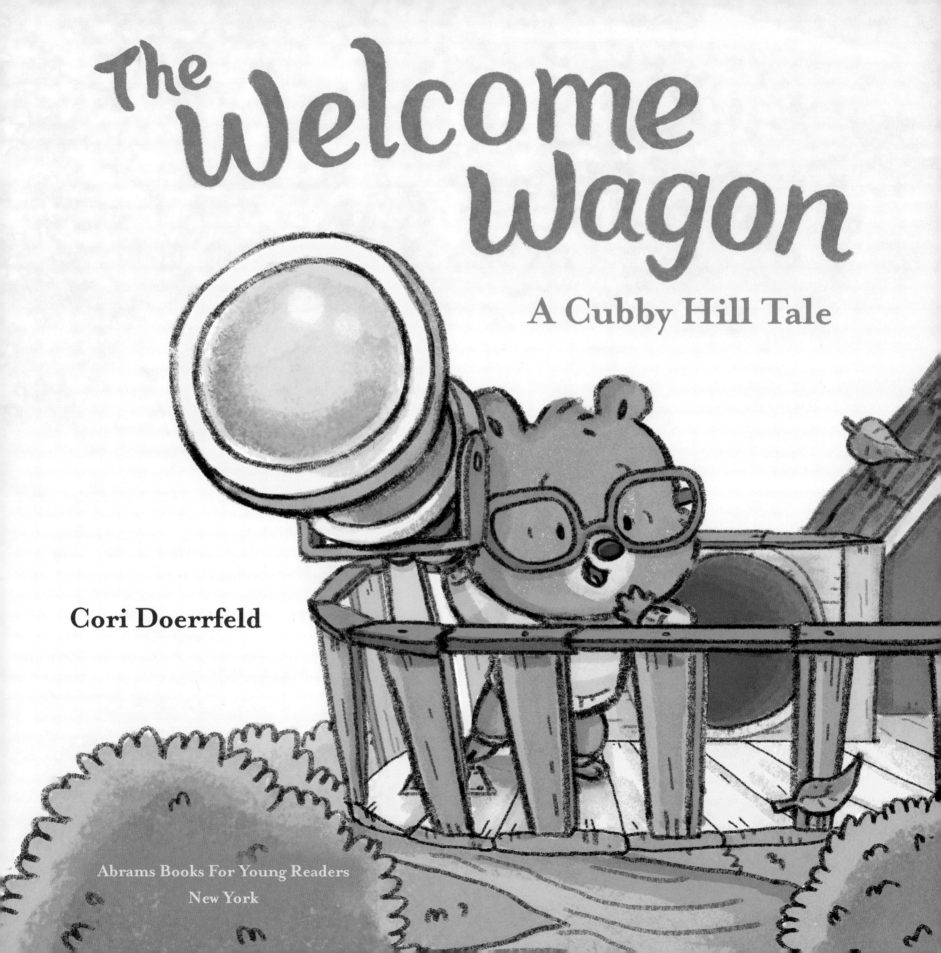

Abrams Books For Young Readers
New York

Cooper was the first to find out.

Beep, beep!
"Bobbi! Someone new is moving to Cubby Hill!"

"Someone *new*?" Bobbi's ears twitched.
"What are they like?"

"I'm not sure yet," said Cooper. "But let's go say hi and give them
a warm Cubby Hill welcome!!"

"Hmmm . . ." Bobbi began to worry. "What if they don't want to meet us?
What if we don't get along?"

Cooper smiled. "Just come with me and see!"

"Oooh!" Henry's spines prickled. "Should I bring them some flowers?"

"That's a great idea!" said Cooper.

"But what if . . ." Bobbi's nose wrinkled. "They're *allergic* to flowers?"

"Really?!" Stella's tail swooshed.
"Can I play video games with them?"

"Sure," said Cooper.
"Bring your favorites!"

"But what if . . ." Bobbi shrugged.
"They don't know *how* to play video games!"

Everyone Cooper drove by made them wonder
what the someone new would be like.

"What do you think they'll look like?" asked Cooper.

"Ooh!" said Henry. "Maybe they're really tall?"

"Or have lots of long hair," added Stella.

"What if . . ." Bobbi chomped.
"They don't look like *anybody* we've ever seen before?"

"Eek!" cried Henry.
"What if they have lots of long *teeth*?"

"Ha!" Cooper shook his head. "Probably not.
But maybe they *sound* different from us!"

"Ah," said Henry, "like maybe they make cute noises!"
"Or speak another language," added Stella.

"What if . . ." Bobbi worried. "They sound like this, *Raaaaaar, raaaaar, rarrrrr!*"
"Oh no," said Stella. "What *if* they make scary noises!"

"Do you really think that could happen?!" Cooper kept on going.
"I want to know if they like to play sports.

"What music they listen to . . ."

". . . or what toppings they eat on their pizza!"
"What if . . ." Bobbi gulped. "They eat something *totally terrifying*!"

"C'mon guys!" Cooper tried to reassure them.
"Don't you want to know who's in their family?

"Where they're from?

"Or if they have cool stuff to show us?"

"What if . . ." Bobbi's ears trembled.
"They're *not* like ANYONE else who's *ever* lived in Cubby Hill!?"

"What if they're from a different planet?!" Henry's spines quivered.
"And they're here to *destroy us all*?!" Stella's tail straightened.

"I think . . ." Cooper waved with a sigh.
"They're just curious to meet us too!"

"Oh!" said Henry. "You're so sweet!"

"And very helpful," said Stella.

"I can't believe I thought you ate bunnies
on your pizza," added Bobbi.

"*Hee-hee!* Of course not!" said Muffin.
"But we do eat cheese on our ice cream. Want to try some?"
"*Squeak!*" said Muggy.

Soon they all realized that someone new isn't just someone to welcome,
they're someone to celebrate!

Because what if they share something you've never seen before?

What if they're full of the most *amazing* ideas?

What if, as Cooper and his friends learned,
they turn out to be the *best* new neighbors ever!